Play with Me!

by Anna Prokos

illustrated by Debbie Palen

RED CHAIR PRESS

It's a quiet day in the backyard.
Bulldog wants to play.

Cat strolls by.
She stops to smell the catnip.

"No flowers!" Bulldog barks.
"You better play with me!"

"You can't make me!" Cat says bravely.
Cat feels scared. But she slowly strolls away.

"Get back here," Bulldog growls.
But Cat keeps going.

Just then, Squirrel scurries down the tree.
"Time for breakfast!" Squirrel says.

"No nuts!" Bulldog barks.
"You better play with me!"

"You can't make me!" Squirrel says bravely.
He feels sad and scampers up a tree.

"Get back here," Bulldog growls.
But Squirrel keeps going.

Just then, Skunk comes strolling by.
"Time for a nap," Skunk yawns.

"No nap!" Bulldog barks.
"You better play with me!"

Skunk feels upset. "Don't snap at me,"
she warns. "I don't want to play now."

Bulldog barks his meanest bark.
"Play with me now!" he snarls.

Skunk doesn't like being bullied.

Uh-oh! Cat and Squirrel smell trouble.
"Stop!" shouts Cat.

"Don't spray!" Squirrel squeaks.

"We don't have to fight," Squirrel says.

"Think of what could happen!" Cat howls.

Bulldog thinks for a minute.

"Sorry! I was wrong!," he says.
Bulldog feels happy now.

"Great!" says Cat.
"Now we will play with you!"
And that's just what the four friends do.

Big Question: How did Bulldog bully the other animals? How did Bulldog's actions make the animals feel?

Big Words:

exclaims: speak suddenly with anger or surprise

scampers: run with quick steps in fear or excitement

scurries: move quickly and with excitement

squeaks: speak with a high excited tone